Setting Goals

Katie Peters

GRL Consultants,
Diane Craig and Monica Marx,
Certified Literacy Specialists

Pull Ahead Readers
People Smarts

Lerner Publications ◆ Minneapolis

Note from a GRL Consultant
This Pull Ahead leveled book has been carefully designed for beginning readers. A team of guided reading literacy experts has reviewed and leveled the book to ensure readers pull ahead and experience success.

Lerner Publications Company
An imprint of Lerner Publishing Group, Inc.
241 First Avenue North
Minneapolis, MN 55401 USA

For reading levels and more information, look up this title at www.lernerbooks.com.

Main body text set in Memphis Pro 24/39
Typeface provided by Linotype.

Photo Acknowledgments
The images in this book are used with the permission of: © AngiePhotos/Getty Images, p. 3; © FatCamera/Getty Images, pp. 12–13; © HRAUN/Getty Images, pp. 8–9, 16 (piano); © JasonDoiy/Getty Images, pp. 14–15; © nilimage/Getty Images, pp. 4–5; © pinstock/Getty Images, pp. 6–7, 16 (vegetables); © RichVintage/Getty Images, pp. 10–11, 16 (helmet).

Front cover: © wavebreakmedia/Shuttrestock Images

Library of Congress Cataloging-in-Publication Data

Names: Peters, Katie, author.
Title: Setting goals / Katie Peters.
Description: Minneapolis : Lerner Publications, [2022] | Series: Helpful habits (pull ahead readers people smarts - nonfiction) | Includes index. | Summary: "Guide young readers to try new things and learn new skills, habits that are important for success and happiness. Pairs with the fiction title Paco Tries"— Provided by publisher.
Identifiers: LCCN 2020014831 (print) | LCCN 2020014832 (ebook) | ISBN 9781728403465 (library binding) | ISBN 9781728423227 (paperback) | ISBN 9781728418384 (ebook)
Subjects: LCSH: Goal (Psychology)—Juvenile literature.
Classification: LCC BF505.G6 P48 2021 (print) | LCC BF505.G6 (ebook) | DDC 155.4/191—dc23

LC record available at https://lccn.loc.gov/2020014831
LC ebook record available at https://lccn.loc.gov/2020014832

Manufactured in the United States of America
1 - 48342 - 48884 - 1/22/2021

Table of Contents

Setting Goals

I will learn a new game.

I will try a new food.

I will learn a new song.

I will try a new sport.

I will learn a new word.

I will try a new job.

What is something you would like to do or learn?

Did You See It?

helmet

piano

vegetables

Index